What Sadie Saw

Dick King-Smith

Scholastic Children's Books,
Commonwealth House, 1-19 New Oxford Street,
London, WC1A 1NU, UK
A division of Scholastic Ltd
London ~ New York ~ Toronto ~ Sydney ~ Auckland
Mexico City ~ New Delhi ~ Hong Kong

First published by Scholastic Ltd, 1997
This edition, 1999

ISBN 0590 19536 0

Typeset by DP Photosetting, Aylesbury, Bucks
Printed by Mackays of Chatham plc, Chatham, Kent

10 9 8 7 6 5 4 3 2 1

Contents

Chapter 1

The First Pictures

It was shortly before her eighth birthday that Sadie first realized her extraordinary gift.

She could see into the future.

There was no warning of it. She went to bed one night a perfectly normal girl, and she woke up knowing – with absolute certainty – two things about the next day.

She lay in bed thinking about this. In the crook of her arm was her favourite old toy, a very battered and threadbare camel called Abdul. Abdul's ears had fallen off and his two humps were all soft and floppy but his beady black eyes were still bright as Sadie told him what had happened.

She told Abdul everything, always had, but never

before anything as exciting as this.

"Listen, Abdul," she said, "and I'll tell you two things about today, two things that I *know* are going to happen. I've got pictures in my mind. One's got something to do with rain – a storm of rain, a thunderstorm, I dare say. And the other is about money – about me finding some money, I think. I'm absolutely sure in my mind about both these things."

Abdul, as was his habit, said nothing.

"I'm only telling all this to you," said Sadie, "not to the rest of the family. It's a secret between you and me, understand?" and the old camel nodded his head up and down several times, possibly because Sadie had hold of his neck and was waggling it.

Sadie was the eldest of the three Makepeace children. Carl was four and a half, and there was a baby called Julia.

At breakfast, Sadie watched her mother ladling food into Julia's gaping, birdlike mouth and said, "Mum, are you going to have another baby?"

"Steady on!" said Mrs Makepeace. "Julia's only ten months old."

"I don't mean straight away," Sadie said. "I mean, are you going to have another one some time?"

"No!" said Mr Makepeace firmly.

"I don't know," said his wife. "And hurry up with your breakfast or we'll be late for school."

Sadie poured milk on to her Rice Krispies and listened to them snapping and crackling and popping. You may not know, Mum, she thought, what's going to happen in the future, but if you wait a while I'll probably be able to tell you if Carl and Julia and I are going to have another brother or sister; at the moment I'm only looking one day ahead, but you never know, I may get better at it.

The day started fine and warm with clear skies, but as she skipped around the playground at morning break, Sadie thought she heard a distant rumble. It was hard to be sure, with all the shouting and yelling the children were making, but halfway through the next lesson there was a sudden dazzle of lightning and then a great clap of thunder that made everyone jump. After that, the rain came down in torrents.

And when school ended, and the three Makepeace

children were on their way home with their mother, Sadie suddenly saw something shining at the edge of the pavement, and she bent and picked up a one-pound coin. That evening she told her camel all about it.

"It all happened," she said, "exactly as I had foreseen, Abdul Pasha."

("Pasha", she had found in a book, was a title given to very important Turkish people. She saw no reason why Abdul should not be a Turkish camel, and he was certainly a very important person.)

"How odd it is," Sadie went on, "to think that when I wake up tomorrow morning, I shall foresee some more things."

But she was wrong. When she woke, she found she had absolutely no knowledge about the day ahead except that it was Saturday.

Funny, Sadie thought. How could I have been so certain about those two things happening? Was it just a fluke?

For ten days or more it seemed that it was, but then one morning Sadie woke up with that same feeling of certainty about what would happen that day.

It wasn't a feeling about something natural, like a thunderstorm, or something nice, like finding a one-pound coin. It was definitely a nasty feeling; something nasty was going to happen, to someone in the family, she didn't know who, she didn't know what.

But once again there was the clearest picture in her mind, a picture of something dripping – drip, drip, drip – down on to the floor. They were bright red, these drips. And they weren't tomato sauce.

Chapter 2

Careful!

"**B**lood!" said Sadie to her camel. "Someone's bleeding. Or they're soon going to be."

Abdul Pasha looked impassive.

Sadie leaped out of bed. Passing the open bathroom door, she saw her father shaving.

Razors are sharp, thought Sadie. They cut you.

"Careful, Dad!" she shouted.

Mr Makepeace jumped. "What d'you think you're up to, Sadie?" he said, turning towards her a face that was angry as well as lathery. "You nearly made me cut myself."

"Sorry," said Sadie, "but mind you don't," and she rushed downstairs.

In the kitchen her mother was cutting bread with a

saw-edged knife. Knives are sharp, thought Sadie. They cut you.

"Look out, Mum!" she called.

Mrs Makepeace gave a start of surprise. "Don't frighten me like that, Sadie," she said. "I might have sliced my finger off."

"Sorry," said Sadie. "Be careful you don't. Where's Carl? Where's Julia?"

"In the sitting-room."

As you might expect in a room of that name, Sadie's brother and sister were both sitting, Carl on the floor cutting out pictures from an old magazine, Julia in her little rocking-chair trying to grab hold of one of the kittens.

The Makepeaces had two black-and-white kittens. One was black but partly white, one was white but mostly black, so of course their names were Partly and Mostly.

Instantly Sadie sensed danger. The scissors looked sharp. They could easily hurt Carl. And if Julia managed to pull Mostly's tail as she was trying to do, he would certainly scratch her. Scissors and kitten could both draw blood.

Quickly Sadie took the scissors from her brother and moved her little sister away from the kitten.

Carl shouted angrily at her, using what he thought was very bad language.

"Filthy stink mess!" he cried.

Julia wailed loudly.

Their mother came in. "Whatever is happening?" she said.

"She took my scissors!" cried Carl, and Julia, who could not yet talk, yelled louder.

Their father came in. "What on earth is going on?" he said.

"Sadie took Carl's scissors away . . ." said his wife.

"They're dangerous," Sadie said. "He could hurt himself."

"... and she's upset Julia, I don't know how..."

"She was teasing Mostly," Sadie said. "He could have scratched her."

"... and before that she gave me such a start I nearly cut myself with the bread knife."

"And I nearly cut myself shaving," said Mr Makepeace, "because she suddenly shouted at me."

"Whatever's the matter with you this morning, Sadie?" they both said.

Sadie glowered at all of them. One of them's going to be bleeding today, she thought, and any of those things could have caused it. What's the use of me foreseeing things if they all just get angry?

"I was only trying to be helpful," she said.

"Helpful?" said Mrs Makepeace.

"Don't be so silly," said Mr Makepeace.

"Give me the scissors!" cried Carl, while Julia yelled more lustily still.

Despite all this, Sadie did not give up. She could not tell them all that one of them was going to shed his or her life-blood – they wouldn't believe her – but she did what she could to warn them. As her father was leaving for work, she said to him in a very solemn tone of voice,

"Daddy, you must drive carefully today."

"I always do," he said. "But why specially today?"

"Oh, I don't know. Just promise you will."

"All right."

And when Mrs Makepeace had left Sadie and Carl at the school gates and was about to set off back home with Julia in the pram, Sadie said, again very seriously, "You will take care today, Mum, won't you?"

"Care of what?"

"Well, mind how you cross the road. And watch out when you're cooking because accidents often happen in the kitchen."

"Goodness!" said her mother. "You're all doom and gloom this morning, aren't you? Why's that?"

"Oh, I don't know," Sadie said, "but do take care of Julia, won't you? And I'll try to keep an eye on Carl."

When the bell went for morning break, Sadie rushed along to the Reception classroom and stood watching as the youngest ones came out to play. Carl looked all right. There were no bandages or plasters on him.

She followed him about in the playground, waiting for him to fall down and scrape his knees or catch his finger on a broken bit of the wire fence. Or, for example, some bigger boy might show Carl his Swiss Army knife and Carl might feel the blade to see how sharp it was.

Those drips of blood were still very clear in her mind. Someone – Mum, Dad, Carl or Julia – was going to shed them before the day was out.

There were fish fingers for lunch, but although she liked it, Sadie could not bring herself to drip blood-red tomato sauce on them as the others were doing.

After lunch, and again at afternoon break, she dogged Carl's footsteps, but he finished the school day undamaged.

Unharmed also, it seemed, were her mother and the baby, and Mr Makepeace drove his car safely home.

Sadie was undaunted, and unceasing in her worry. It would happen to one of them this evening then, whatever it was; she was sure of it, she had foreseen it, it *must* happen.

"It *must*," she said to her camel (and his head moved up and down). But then a thought struck her.

"It doesn't have to be human blood," she said. "It could be cat blood, Abdul Pasha! It could be an accident happening to Partly or Mostly!" And she dashed out of her room to hurry downstairs and make sure the kittens were all right.

She was in such a rush that she missed her footing at

the head of the stairs and tumbled all the way down them.

At the sound her parents came hurrying out into the hall.

"Have you hurt yourself?" they cried.

Sadie got to her feet. "I banged by dose on sub-thing," she said.

"You certainly did," said her mother.

"Poor old girl," said her father, as the bright red blood dripped – drip, drip, drip – from Sadie's nose down on to the floor.

Chapter 3

The Umbrella

Sadie's next piece of second-sight happened at the weekend. As soon as she woke, she told Abdul Pasha what was clearly in her mind.

"I don't think it's anything nasty this time," she said to him. "At least I hope not. It isn't a proper picture of something happening, you see; it's just two words. But I can't make any sense of them." She picked up the old camel by his curved neck and stared into his eyes.

" 'Down Under'," she said. "Those are the two words. Does that mean anything to you?" She moved her hand and Abdul shook his head.

"Down under what?" she said, and she slid out of bed and looked beneath it.

There was quite a lot of fluff and dust, an old comic

that must have slipped over the back of the bed, a china pot that she had never even known was there, and a white chamber pot with a pattern of pink roses.

"Perhaps the pot's got something to do with 'down under'," she said to Abdul. "Or maybe it's something down under my bedroom. Let's see, what's below here? The kitchen, isn't it?"

She couldn't see anything out of the ordinary in the kitchen. She looked down under the kitchen table, to see the two kittens, each eating from his dish in that picky way that cats have. Mostly had partly finished his breakfast, Partly's was still mostly uneaten.

Her mother came in to find Sadie looking in all the cupboards beneath the work surfaces.

"Lost something?" she said.

"Sort of," Sadie said.

The front doorbell rang twice.

"Postman," said Mrs Makepeace. "Fetch it, Sadie, will you?"

Sadie picked up the letters from the mat and glanced through them without much interest – she never got any letters though a stamp on one of them did catch her eye. It bore a picture of a leaping kangaroo. It was addressed to her father.

As he went through his mail at breakfast time, he suddenly said, "Hullo, here's one from Down Under."

Sadie looked up quickly. The envelope her father was slitting open was the one with the kangaroo stamp.

"Must be from your cousin Beryl," Mrs Makepeace said.

All at the same time Julia said her first and as yet only word, "More!" while Carl said, "What's a cousin?" and Sadie said, "What did you mean, Dad, when you said 'one from Down Under'?"

Her mother stuffed a spoon into Julia's mouth and said to Carl, "She's the daughter of Daddy's uncle," and Mr Makepeace said to Sadie, "Down Under means Australia or New Zealand. In this case, Australia."

Sadie felt a bit disappointed. That was all her second-sight meant then. Just a letter from some old cousin in Australia. Boring. But her father didn't seem to find the letter boring.

"Blimey!" he said to his wife. "Listen to this, Jill."

Dear Brian (he read),

I'm sorry to have to tell you that my father has recently died — a merciful release really, as he'd been very ill with no hope of recovery.

As you know, I think, I am your uncle Jim's only child and so his sole heir. Which means that I am now able to afford — amongst other things — a holiday in the UK which is something I've long wanted to do. We left when I was small and I've never been back.

I don't want to impose myself upon you and your wife, but it would be nice to see you again, and Jill and the children, none of whom of course I've ever met. I don't think you and I have seen each other for about thirty years! My flight arrives at Heathrow at midday on July 1st. I know you live fairly near. May I ring you from the airport?

> *Love to all the family,*
> *Beryl*

"July the first!" cried Mrs Makepeace. "That's less than a week away. What on earth are we going to do, Brian? To start with, we've no spare bedroom."

"She could have my room," said Sadie. "I could go on a camp bed in Carl's room."

"Don't want you in my room," said Carl. "You'd keep me awake."

"That's very nice of you, Sadie love," said her mother, "but I think it might be better if you stay where you are, and we'll move Julia's cot in with Daddy and me."

"Don't want Julia in our room," said Mr Makepeace. "I'd never get a wink of sleep."

"If I did go into Carl's room," said Sadie, "and you let me stay up a bit later at night – just while Daddy's cousin's here – then Carl would be asleep by the time I went to bed, so I wouldn't disturb him."

"Good idea," said her father.

"Well, all right then," said her mother.

"Stink!" said her brother.

"More!" said her sister.

On the morning of July the first Sadie woke up with a very definite picture in her head. It was a complete picture of Cousin Beryl, waiting at the airport. She

knew it was Cousin Beryl because the picture was so clear that she could even see the name on the label of one of the suitcases standing beside her.

Beryl Makepeace, it said.

(So she can't be married, Sadie thought, or she'd have changed her name.)

The person she could see in her mind's eye was not tall – rather short, in fact – or slender – a bit tubby indeed – and she had a mop of curly black hair. But the thing that Sadie noticed particularly about her was that she was carrying a large rolled-up umbrella, sloped over her shoulder like a soldier's rifle. It was one of those coloured golf umbrellas, striped red, yellow and green.

At breakfast there was a discussion about who should go to the airport when Cousin Beryl rang.

"We could all go, I suppose," said Mr Makepeace doubtfully. "Though I think that might be a bit much for Beryl; she'll be pretty tired anyway."

"More!" said Julia loudly.

"She will," his wife said, spooning food into the baby, "and anyway I've got too much to do, getting lunch ready and everything, and I wouldn't want to lug Julia up to Heathrow anyway. You go on your own, Brian."

"I hope I shall recognize her," Mr Makepeace said. "I think we were each about five when I last saw her. I've no idea what she looks like."

I have, Sadie thought. I could tell you exactly.

"I expect that when she rings, she'll say she'll be wearing a flower in her coat or something," said Mrs Makepeace.

"Or carrying an umbrella," Sadie said.

Her mother and father laughed.

"Very sensible thing," her father said, "for an Australian to bring on holiday in this country."

"Why?" said Carl.

"Well, it rains quite a lot here, doesn't it?"

"It's not raining today," said Carl.

"No, it's a lovely day."

"Then she won't have an umbrella," said Carl.

"No. Of course not. You're quite right."

"More!" said Julia.

"Anyway," said Mr Makepeace, "let's all have a guess at what Beryl will be like. All I can remember of her as a child is that she was dark haired."

"But she might have turned blonde," said his wife. "I think of all Australians as blonde. I say she'll have very fair hair, and she'll be tall and slim."

"I've got an idea Uncle Jim was quite tall," said her husband, "so I'll say Beryl will be tall too, and perhaps quite a big sort of a woman if you know what I mean. But dark haired. What do you guess, Carl?"

Carl stared at his father. He knew that this person who was arriving was his father's cousin, and cousins, he supposed, looked pretty much alike.

"She'll look just exactly like you, Daddy," he said.

"Well then, she will be tall and fair," said his mother.

"And she'll have a moustache," said Sadie.

Her parents laughed.

"Foul stink!" said Carl crossly.

"More!" said Julia.

"Your turn now, Sadie," said her father. "What do you think Cousin Beryl will look like?"

Sadie screwed up her face and pretended to be thinking furiously. "Well," she said at last, "she won't be tall. She'll be rather short. And she won't be thin. She'll be quite plump. And yes, she will be dark haired; very curly hair it will be."

"Okay," said her father. "Anything else?"

"Yes," Sadie said. "She *will* be carrying an umbrella, a stripy one – red, yellow and green."

Her father laughed. "Quite an imagination!" he said.

But when at about half-past twelve the phone rang and Mr Makepeace had answered it, he called to his wife, "Jill! Can you come here a minute?" and when she did so, "That was Beryl. She's just arrived."

"Did she say how to recognize her?"

"Yes. Where's Sadie?"

"Out in the garden. Why? What's the matter? You look as if you've had a shock."

"I have. It's really weird. Beryl said, 'You can't miss me, Brian, I'm short and tubby, with curly dark hair.'"

"So Sadie was right," said Mrs Makepeace. "Nothing specially amazing about that. It was just a guess."

"But that's not all," replied Mr Makepeace. "The other thing Beryl said was that she'd be carrying an umbrella with red, yellow and green stripes."

Chapter 4

Just a Guess

"I bought it," said Cousin Beryl, "as a sort of talisman. You know, not just to keep the rain off, but to keep it from raining at all during my holiday. You get much more of the stuff than we do."

Mr Makepeace had met his cousin at Terminal 4 at Heathrow and brought her home, and she had been introduced to his wife and the three children and Partly and Mostly.

"How long are you over here for?" asked Mrs Makepeace.

"Four whole lovely weeks," said Cousin Beryl. "Which reminds me, Brian, I need to contact a car-hire firm. I'm planning to drive all over the place – to Bath, to Stratford-on-Avon, the Lake District, the Highlands of Scotland, the Yorkshire Dales. There's no limit to the places I want to see if I can."

"Aren't you going to stay with us at all?" Sadie said.

"We very much hope you will," said her mother, whose face had fallen at the mention of four weeks and whose spirits had then risen on hearing of the hire-car.

"Well, I'd like to stay tonight and tomorrow night if I could," said Cousin Beryl, "and then set off on Monday morning. And perhaps I could spend my last night with you before I fly home? But have you got room for me?"

"Oh, yes," said Sadie quickly. "You're going in my room."

"But where will you sleep, Sadie?"

"In Carl's room. On a camp bed. He won't mind."

"I will," Carl said.

"Look," said Cousin Beryl. "I don't want to turn Sadie out of her bed. I used to do a lot of camping when I was her age. Why don't I sleep on the camp bed?"

"In my room?" said Carl. He sounded horrified.

"No. In Sadie's room. If she wouldn't mind."

"I don't mind a bit," said Sadie. "Then I could stay up really really late."

"Why?" asked her mother.

"Well, Cousin Beryl wouldn't disturb me when she came to bed because I'd still be awake."

Her mother smiled. "You can forget that," she said.

Her father smiled. "Nice try," he said.

Beryl smiled. "I shall be early to bed tonight anyway," she said. "I'm jet-lagged. And don't bother with the 'cousin', Sadie – just call me Beryl."

"At breakfast this morning," Mrs Makepeace said, "we were playing a game, guessing what you would look like, Beryl."

"And Sadie had you figured out exactly," said Mr Makepeace.

Husband and wife looked at one another, and each knew that neither was going to say anything about the red, yellow and green striped umbrella. Not yet, anyway. It must, each thought, have just been the most extraordinary coincidence. How could Sadie have possibly known?

"How did you know what I looked like, Sadie?" said Beryl.

Sadie grinned. "It's a secret," she said.

Beryl grinned. "Perhaps she'll tell me," she said to the others, "when we have long talks in the middle of the night."

"Can we?" said Sadie.

"No!" said everyone.

When Sadie did go to bed that evening (a bit later than she usually did) she lay awake for some time, thinking about her cousin. Beryl had explained the relationship to her.

"My father and your grandfather were brothers, so your daddy and I are first cousins, so you and I are first cousins once removed," she said.

And Beryl *was* once removed, thought Sadie – to Australia. But now she's here, and that's nice because I like her. I'm sorry her father died but then old people always do die, and I'm glad he left her a lot of money because she didn't have enough to come here before. I wonder if I shall foresee anything about her holiday? And if I do, whether I should tell her? And should I tell her about the other things I've already foreseen? And what shall I say if Mum and Dad ask me how I knew about the umbrella? I'll say I dreamt it. Perhaps I did dream it. Perhaps I dreamt all those things. But I can't remember dreaming them. I just woke up and they were there. Can you have dreams without knowing you've had them? I'll ask Beryl. I must stay awake till she comes to bed.

But when Beryl did come to bed (a lot earlier than she usually did) Sadie was fast asleep.

When she opened her eyes the following morning,

Sadie's first thought, as always, was of what she now called her "pictures". Was there one in her mind, today, of something in the future? No. All she knew about was the past, yesterday in particular, when her cousin had arrived from the other side of the world.

She turned on to her tummy, quietly so as not to wake the shape in the camp bed at the other side of the room, and thought about Australia.

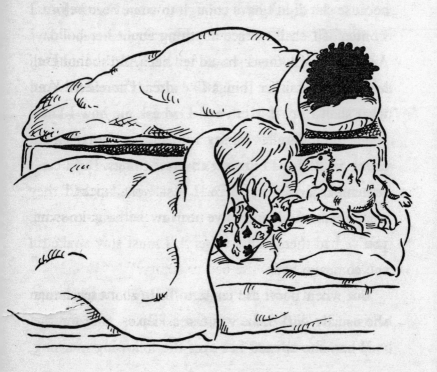

The quickest way to get there would be straight down, down through the bed, through the china pot beneath it, through the floor, down into the kitchen, down through the foundations of the house and on down into the earth, deeper and deeper, for thousands of miles, getting hotter and hotter, right into the red-hot middle of the world, and then keeping on going, getting cooler now, for thousands more miles until you would suddenly pop out (upside down, of course) into the fresh air once again. Down Under.

I wonder if I'll ever go to Australia, Sadie thought. Beryl might ask me one day, when I'm older. You never know.

Then the shape in the camp bed turned over and a voice said, "Good morning, Sadie."

"Hullo," Sadie said. "Did you sleep all right?"

"So-so," Beryl said. "I've been awake for quite some time."

"Oh. Sorry. Was the bed uncomfy?"

"No, no, it's just the jet-lag. We're about ten hours behind you back home, you see. Takes time for the body-clock to adjust."

Sadie sat up in bed, holding Abdul.

"Who's that?" said Beryl.

"My camel. Abdul Pasha. He's Turkish."

"How delightful," said Beryl. "We have wild camels in Australia, in the outback. Perhaps you'll see them one day."

"I don't suppose I'll ever go there," said Sadie.

"You might. When you're older. You never know. How old is Abdul Pasha?"

"He's ever so old. Daddy had him when he was a little boy."

"That's when I last saw your dad."

"Well, perhaps Abdul met you when he was young. Did you, Abdul?" Sadie asked, and the old camel nodded.

"What a nice thought," said Beryl. "Do you talk to him a lot?"

"Oh, yes. I tell him about things that have happened."

"What about things that are going to happen? In the future, I mean."

Why did she say that? Sadie thought.

"How could I tell him what was going to happen?" she said. "People can't see into the future."

"Some people can," said Beryl.

"Do you believe that?"

"Oh, yes. But I only meant that, for instance you, might have mentioned to Abdul that I'm going to hire a car today. Has she told you that, Abdul Pasha?"

The camel shook his head.

"I wonder what sort of car it will be," said Beryl. "And what colour. Now, if only you had the gift of second-sight, Sadie, you could tell me the answer."

Oh, if only I'd woken up with a picture of the car, Sadie thought, but I haven't a clue. I could have a guess though. No harm in that.

"Actually," she said, "I have got second-sight."

Beryl smiled. "Go on then," she said.

Red's the commonest colour, Sadie thought. You see more red cars. And you see masses of Fords. And lots of them are hatchbacks.

"The car that you will hire for your holiday, Beryl," she said in a very confident voice, "will be a red Ford hatchback."

"That's settled then," said Beryl.

Later that morning, as Mr Makepeace was setting off to drive his cousin to the car-hire firm, Beryl wound down the window and said, "By the way, Jill, I already know exactly what car I am going to hire."

"How?" said Mrs Makepeace.

"Oh, Sadie told me. She can foresee the future, she says."

Husband and wife glanced at one another.

"Oh, really?" said Mr Makepeace. "And what did she say you would choose?"

"A red Ford hatchback."

Later still, when her husband returned, Sadie's mother lost no time in asking, "Did Beryl manage to hire a car?"

"Yes."

"Was it...?"

"Look outside," said Mr Makepeace. "She was just behind me. She's parking it now."

Mrs Makepeace ran to the window, to see Beryl getting out of a white Vauxhall saloon.

Chapter 5

Pile-up

"I was wrong," Sadie said, when next she had a chance to speak to Beryl alone.

"It was only a guess, wasn't it?" said Beryl with a smile.

"Yes."

"So when you told me you had second-sight, you were fibbing?"

"No. You see, I didn't just know what you would look like, I knew you would have a striped umbrella. Before Daddy met you at the airport, I mean. I saw a picture of it all, in my mind."

"Colours too?"

"Yes, red, yellow and green. I expect they didn't tell you that because they thought it was spooky. They'll be happier now that I got the car all wrong, but, like you said, I was only guessing. I didn't have any picture of it."

"Have you had other pictures before?" Beryl asked.

"Yes. Of a storm of rain and of me finding some money. Both of those happened. And of blood dripping."

"Oh, dear. And did that happen too?"

"Yes, it did. I fell down the stairs and got a nosebleed. And then a little bit later I saw these two words –
Down Under – and then your letter arrived."

"And then you saw the picture of me with the
umbrella?"

"Yes," said Sadie. "So you believe me?" she asked.

"Yes, Sadie, I do," said Beryl. "You probably don't
know, but I'm a psychiatrist."

"What does that mean?"

"It means among other things that I'm very interested in what goes on in people's minds. There are all
sorts of things that you're not aware of going on inside
your brain. Perhaps when I come back at the end of my
holiday, you'll tell me if you've seen any more pictures?"

Sadie nodded.

"When you see these pictures, is it always at the
same time of day?" asked Beryl.

"Yes. First thing when I wake up in the morning."

"Perhaps you'll see one tomorrow. Before I go."

"I can't promise," Sadie said.

"No, but you could promise not to tell me any more made-up ones, like the hire-car."

"That was silly," Sadie said. "I won't do that again."

The rest of that Sunday was very nice, Sadie thought. Beryl seemed to fit in so well with the family. Mum and Dad obviously liked her, and Carl actually offered her some of his sweets (which he never normally did to anyone), and Julia allowed her to spoon-feed her (which she would actually have allowed anyone to do), and Partly and Mostly leaped into her lap and held purring competitions.

"I wish Beryl was staying with us for the whole four weeks," Sadie said to her mother that evening. "Don't you?"

"That might be rather boring for her. Don't forget she's seen nothing of this country. She's got all sorts of places she wants to visit."

"Where's she going tomorrow, Mum?"

"To Bath."

"How d'you get there?"

"Down the M4. And talking of baths, it's time you had one."

"You look nice and clean," her father said when she came downstairs later in her dressing-gown. Julia was asleep in her cot, Carl was asleep in his bed, the kittens were asleep in their basket.

"Did you know," Beryl said, "that there would have been something different if you'd been having a bath in Australia?"

"What?" said Sadie.

"Well, did you watch the water going down the plug-hole?"

"No."

"If you had, you'd have seen that it spins round clockwise as it goes down. In Australia it spins round anticlockwise. Remember that, if you ever take a trip Down Under."

Later, after Sadie had cleaned her teeth (and watched the toothpasty water spinning down clockwise), she lay in bed, wishing that Beryl wasn't going to drive away down the M4 tomorrow. Then she began to feel sleepy, so she turned on her side and arranged Abdul Pasha so that his old head was on the pillow beside her, and said goodnight to him, and fell fast asleep. She did not hear her cousin come to bed, and could not know that Beryl lay awake for some time, thinking about her and her pictures.

But when Sadie woke next morning, there was the clearest of pictures in her mind.

It was a motorway, that was plain; she could even see a sign with M4 written on it. It was a still picture; none of the cars and lorries were moving, but the ones facing towards her were all in their orderly lanes, the slow, the middle and the fast.

But on the other side there was a very different scene. Cars, vans, lorries, coaches were scattered right across the three lanes, all facing different ways, and many, it was clear, had smashed into others. There was one car, right in the middle of the pile-up, that looked more bashed-up than any. It was a white car.

Somehow Sadie made herself keep quiet until she saw that Beryl was awake, and then she said, "Beryl, you mustn't go to Bath today, you simply mustn't!"

"You've seen a picture, have you?" Beryl asked.

"Yes. There's going to be an awful pile-up on the M4."

"What time are you setting off, Beryl?" said Mr Makepeace at breakfast.

"How long will it take me to get to Bath?" Beryl asked.

"Hour and three quarters, two hours at the most. Straight down the M4."

"What's the motorway speed limit in this country?"

"Seventy miles an hour," said Mrs Makepeace.

"Do a hundred miles an hour!" shouted Carl. "Vroom! Vroom!"

"More!" cried Julia.

None of them saw Beryl look towards Sadie and give a little wink.

That Monday evening when Mr Makepeace arrived home from work, he said to his wife, "Did Beryl get off all right?"

"Yes, she left about ten. She said she might give us a ring from Bath."

"Right. Let's watch the early evening news then."

"Can I watch, Daddy?" asked Sadie.

"If you like."

At the start of the news the newscaster said, "This morning there was yet another motorway pile-up. It happened at about eleven o'clock on the westbound carriageway of the M4 as a result of what the police describe as a further example of motorway madness. A large number of vehicles were involved."

Then followed a picture of cars, vans, lorries and coaches braking and swerving and colliding with one another, and ending up scattered right across all three lanes in a series of multiple crashes. Worst crushed of all was a white car that might well have been a Vauxhall saloon.

Sadie's mother and father leant forward in horror, gripping the arms of their chairs. Only Sadie looked quite unworried.

The phone rang, and Mr Makepeace hurried to answer it.

"Who was it?" cried Mrs Makepeace when he returned. "Was it the police? Or a hospital?"

"No. It was Beryl."

"Is she all right?"

"Yes."

"Oh, thank goodness! Then it wasn't her in that white car?"

"No."

"Did she see the pile-up? On her way to Bath, I mean."

"No. She wasn't even on the M4. She went by the old A4 instead – you know, via Reading and Newbury and Marlborough and Chippenham."

"Why ever . . .? That's miles longer. Why didn't she go by the motorway?"

"She said a little bird told her not to."

Chapter 6

More Pictures

That night Sadie's mother and father were talking – about Beryl, about the M4 crash, about Sadie.

"She said to Beryl that she could foresee the future," said her father. "I'm surprised she didn't know that that pile-up was going to happen."

"Oh, that's all childish nonsense," said her mother, "pretending to be clever in that sort of way. If you remember, she also told Beryl that she would hire a red Ford hatchback. It's just a guessing game."

"Yes, of course," said Mr Makepeace. "Though I must say that business about Beryl's umbrella was very strange. Sadie even had the colours right. She probably dreamt it. I can just about believe that it's possible to dream about things that haven't yet happened. But for a child to pretend to be clairvoyant is silly."

His wife nodded in agreement.

Nonetheless she took the chance, catching Sadie on her own the next day, to bring up the subject.

"It doesn't look as though Beryl will need her umbrella today," she said.

"No," said Sadie. "It's nice and sunny, here anyway."

"Funny, you guessing exactly what colours there were on that umbrella."

"Yes, wasn't it?"

"How did you know?"

"Must have dreamt it."

And at the end of the day Sadie's father, also catching her on her own, went through the same rigmarole and got the same answer.

Neither parent told the other.

For a while Sadie saw no more pictures. After a week or so Beryl telephoned. She'd been in the Lake District, she said, and was heading for the Highlands. At the end of the conversation she asked if she could have a word with Sadie.

"Sure," said Mr Makepeace. "Sadie, come and speak to Beryl."

"Hullo," Sadie said.

"Hullo, Sadie," said Beryl. "Listen, I'm just going to ask you questions that you can answer 'Yes' or 'No' to. Okay?"

"Yes."

"First of all of course, there's the business of the M4 pile-up. I reckon I may have been very lucky to have you for a cousin. Did you tell your parents you'd warned me about it?"

"No."

"Have you seen any more pictures?"

"No."

"If you do, you will remember to write them down for me, won't you?"

"Yes."

"Right. You're quite well, are you?"

"Yes."

"And Carl and Julia?"

"Yes."

"And Partly and Mostly?"

"Yes."

"And Abdul Pasha?"

"Yes."

"Good. I'll send you a postcard from the Highlands. Goodbye for now."

"Goodbye," Sadie said.

"That was a good old chat you had," said her father. "I counted six yesses and two noes. What was she saying to you?"

"Just asking how everyone was," said Sadie.

The very next morning she woke up with a picture in her head. It was a brightly-lit room. On one wall, she could see, was a large clock that said 6.30. In the centre of this room was an operating table. Around it stood people wearing gowns and masks. The overhead lights glinted on the sharp scalpel that one of the people held in his hand, and shone on the unconscious figure that lay upon the table. It was the figure of a black-and-white kitten!

Whether it was partly white or mostly black she could not be sure, but it was one or other of them. Some dreadful accident was going to happen to either Partly or Mostly!

Would the vet be able to save his life, whichever one it was? But I could save it, Sadie thought. I could tell Mum and Dad that one of the kittens was going to have an accident, probably get run over on the road, I expect, and then they could keep them safe indoors and it wouldn't happen.

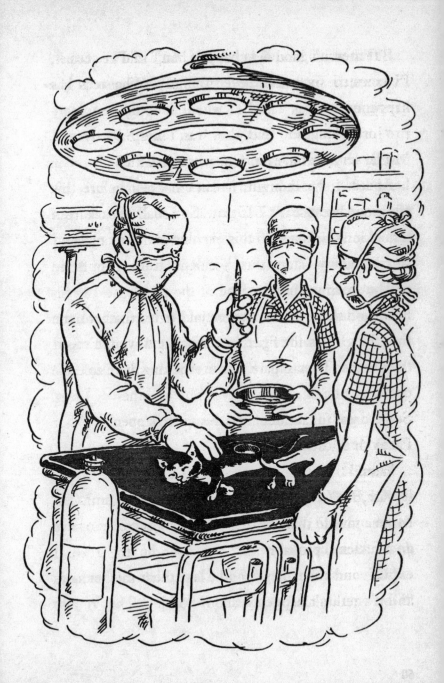

But then it's bound to happen, isn't it? I've seen it. I've seen the picture and everything I've seen so far has happened, so this will. But when? It could be tomorrow or even later, and they can't keep Partly and Mostly shut in for ever. Oh, what shall I do?

At least, she thought, it can't happen before this afternoon because it's 7.15 now. So I shall be back from school long before 6.30 this evening and then maybe I can somehow stop this accident from happening without telling Mum or Dad.

But when her mother collected her from school, the first thing she said to her was, "By the way, don't feed the kittens. They mustn't have anything at all to eat."

"Why not?"

"I've got to take them to the vet this evening."

"Both of them?"

"Yes."

"Oh, no!" cried Sadie. "Will they live, Mum? Can they be saved? What was it? Were they run over or did dogs attack them or what?"

"Of course they'll live, Sadie love," her mother said. "Don't get in such a stew about nothing. They're just going to have a simple little operation, to neuter them, so that they won't grow up to be noisy smelly old tomcats. They'll be as right as rain tomorrow."

"Thank goodness for that," said Sadie to Abdul Pasha that night. She was sitting up in bed with a pad and a pen.

Dear Beryl, she wrote, and then she realized she didn't have Beryl's address. And putting *Beryl Makepeace, The Highlands, Scotland* wouldn't be much use.

"Would it?" she asked the camel, and he shook his head. Instead she wrote,

BERYL. MY PICTURES.

Number 1. I saw one of the kittens on the operating table at the vet's but it was all right, they were both being newtered.

A few days later she received a picture of a different kind. All the Makepeaces had postcards from Beryl.

Sadie's mother and father had one with a view of Inverness Castle; Carl had one with a picture of a black-and-white kitten that looked partly like Partly and mostly like Mostly; and Julia had one that said Happy Birthday, with a picture of a big iced birthday cake (which she tried to eat). *I know it's not your birthday, Julia, but I wonder if you'll try to eat this picture anyway?* Beryl had written on it.

(It's not just me that's got second-sight, Sadie said to herself.)

Sadie's postcard was a reproduction of a photograph. It showed a stretch of water from the centre of which rose a long curved black shape like a giraffe's neck, with a small head on the end of it. Under the photo was written, *The Loch Ness Monster (the Surgeon's Photograph).* On the back Beryl had written, *Here is a picture from the past. Will they ever prove there is a monster in Loch Ness? To know that, you'd have to be able to see into the future. Love from Beryl*

"What does she say?" Sadie's mother asked, and Sadie handed her the postcard.

"She's pulling your leg, Sadie," her mother said, "because of what you said to her."

"But there might be a monster," Sadie said.

"There'd need to be a colony of them," her father

The Loch Ness Monster
(The Surgeon's Photograph)

said. "There couldn't be just one. You'd have to have lots, so that they could breed and produce little monsters."

"More!" shouted Julia.

"Like you," her father said.

Sadie took the Surgeon's Photograph to bed that

night. She showed it to Abdul Pasha but he didn't seem particularly interested.

"It looks very like a monster to me," she said. "Perhaps Beryl will see it while she's up there. And then she could take a photo of it, a better one than this picture. Just imagine the headlines, and then they'd show what she'd filmed. The Psychiatrist's Photograph, it would be called.

How famous Beryl Makepeace would be! How lovely it would be if Sadie Makepeace woke up tomorrow with a picture in her head of Beryl Makepeace taking a picture of the Loch Ness Monster!

Before she settled down to sleep, she stared very hard at the postcard, trying to make such a thing happen. But it didn't.

Nothing in the way of pictures came to Sadie for the rest of that term, and it wasn't till her holidays had begun and Beryl's holiday was half over that Sadie foresaw anything else.

It was a picture of herself standing at the open front door of their house and being handed a parcel by the postman. On the parcel was written, *Sadie, Carl and Julia Makepeace*, and then their address.

The Makepeaces' postman had his own special code, which they knew. If he rang the bell twice, that just meant "I've put the letters through the letter-box. They'll be lying on the mat." But if he gave four rings, that meant, "I've got a parcel for you which is too big to go through the letter-box so I'm waiting for you to open the door."

That morning Sadie waited for the postman to ring as she ate her breakfast. Usually when he did, someone said, "Fetch it, Sadie, would you?" because this was something she liked doing.

Four rings today, she said to herself confidently. But there were only two. And it was the same the next couple of days. Not until the fourth day after her last picture did the postman ring four times. When Sadie went to open the front door, he handed her a parcel with the names of the three children on it.

"It's for me and Carl and Julia," she said to her mother and father.

"I want to open it," Carl said.

"I'm the eldest," Sadie said.

"She always says that!" shouted Carl. "How can I get older than what she is? It's not fair! Foul stink!"

"Let him open it, just this once," Sadie's mother said. "You cut the string and then let him take off the paper."

"All right," said Sadie.

Happy now, Carl tore off the wrapping, and there was a large brightly-coloured tin with EDINBURGH ROCK written on it. On it too was stuck a label that said WITH LOVE FROM BERYL.

Inside the tin were packed lots of sticks of the special grooved rock, all of different pastel shades – pink, pale green, yellow, sandy-coloured and bluish.

"Edinburgh Rock!" said Mr Makepeace. "Haven't

seen any for ages. I used to love that when I was small."

"So did I," said his wife.

And so, it was soon plain, did their children.

After they had finished their breakfast, each was allowed one stick. Sadie ate hers as slowly as possible, Carl ate his as fast as he could, and Julia licked at hers in a slobbery way.

"Is it nice?" her mother asked her, which encouraged Julia to produce her second word.

"Nice!" she said, and then, for luck, "More nice!"

That night Sadie added to BERYL. MY PICTURES.

Number 2. I saw a picture of your parcel arriving and the postman giving it to me. But I did not know what was in it. I saw the picture on a Monday and the parcel did not come till the Thursday so now I can see three days into the future. I wonder what Number 3 will be.

Chapter 7

At the Zoo

When Sadie saw her next picture, she wrote it down straight away. She had no idea what it meant.

"But," she said to Abdul Pasha, "I'll write it down and wait for it to happen."

So she wrote, *Number 3. I saw an elephant.*

A week later, when at breakfast time the postman rang (twice), Sadie went to fetch the post. There were only two things – a letter for her father and a postcard, for all of them, from Beryl. On the card, she could see, was a photograph of an elephant. That's all my last picture was then, thought Sadie – just foreseeing that we'd get a card from Beryl.

"A card from Beryl," her father said when Sadie had

handed him the post.

"Where's she got to?" asked Sadie's mother.

"She's back in London. 'I'm staying here for a couple of days,' she says (there's an address and a phone number for us to contact her), 'seeing all the sights. May I come to you on Saturday 29th for the night? My flight leaves on the 30th. I'll come earlyish, if that's all right, so as to have the whole day with you.' Is that Okay with you, Jill?"

"Fine," Sadie's mother said.

Her husband slit open his letter. "Blimey!" he said.

"What is it, Brian?"

"D'you remember I bought some raffle tickets at that fête we went to earlier in the summer? In aid of some wildlife fund, it was."

"Yes. Don't tell me you've won something?"

"I haven't," said Mr Makepeace, "but if you recall, I bought five tickets, one for each of us, and one of us has won a prize."

"Who?"

"Sadie!"

"Me?" said Sadie.

"Yes. It's not the first prize, nor even the second or third – they're things like holidays abroad or weekends in posh hotels. You've won the fourth prize. I think you'll like it."

"What is it?" Sadie asked.

"The fourth prize", said her father, "is 'Washing an Elephant at the Zoo'."

Is that why Beryl chose that postcard? Sadie thought. Has she got second-sight too?

"Saturday, July 29th," said Mr Makepeace. "That's your Elephant-Washing Day, it says. At 10 a.m."

"But that's the day Beryl's arriving back here, earlyish, she said."

"Why don't we ring her up," said Sadie's mother, "and ask her to meet us at the zoo? Then she can come back with us afterwards."

"What a good idea," said her husband.

So they did.

On the evening of July 28th Sadie added to BERYL. MY PICTURES. So that it now read,

Number 3. I saw an elephant. Then a week later we had a card from you with an elephant on it. And now tomorrow I am going to the zoo to wash an elephant.

At ten o'clock next morning Sadie and her brother and sister and her parents and their cousin Beryl were

all waiting outside the elephant's enclosure at the zoo. With them was the director of the zoo, and the elephant keeper, and quite a crowd of curious onlookers.

On the other side of the moat which surrounded her pen the elephant stood, sideways on to them, shifting her weight from one great cushioned forefoot to the other, her trunk swinging gently from side to side, her little piggy eyes glinting. In front of her forelegs were two large buckets full of water.

Have I got to go in there and throw those over her? Sadie thought worriedly. The animal did look awfully big.

But then the keeper unrolled a hosepipe with a long nozzle on its end, and gave it to Sadie to hold.

"Hold on tight to it, young lady," he said. "It's a powerful hose. And when I turn the water on, you just squirt it all over her, head, body, legs, everywhere. She loves a good wash."

"What are the buckets for?" Sadie asked.

"Well," said the keeper, "this elephant always likes to finish the job off herself. So when you've done your stuff, she'll give herself a good shower bath."

Now the director of the zoo came forward with a plastic cape. "Half a tick," he said. "Let me slip this over you, just in case you get splashed."

Then the keeper put the nozzle of the hose in Sadie's hands and said, "Hold tight now."

"Stand well back, please, everyone else," said the director. "This is Sadie's big moment." And to the keeper he said, "Switch on."

As the jet of water hit the elephant's side and splashed off the thick grey hide, all the watchers clapped (except Carl, who yelled with excitement and Julia, who howled with dismay) at the sight of the small girl squirting water all over the enormous animal.

Holding the powerful hose with both hands, Sadie played it over one side of the elephant, who rocked to and fro, obviously enjoying being washed. Then the keeper shouted a command and the elephant turned about, slowly and deliberately, so that Sadie could hose down the other side.

For perhaps five minutes, for the first and only time in her life, Sadie washed an elephant, until at last the keeper switched off the water.

For a moment the great beast stood, quietly dripping. Then she dipped her trunk into the first of the two full buckets and sucked up the contents and sprayed the water over her own head, while everyone laughed, even Julia.

Sadie caught the creature's piggy eye. It seemed to be looking straight at her. Just for a second it closed, in what looked almost like a wink. Then the elephant put her trunk into the second bucket and sucked up all the water and, stretching out her trunk, carefully squirted the whole lot over Sadie's head, while everyone laughed, except Sadie.

"Did you see the look in that elephant's eye?" said Beryl later to the others. "She thought it was really funny, you could tell!" She smiled at Sadie. "You didn't foresee that, did you?" she said.

Chapter 8

You Never Know

That afternoon Sadie saw that Beryl was sitting all by herself in the garden, reading a book, so she took the chance to show her BERYL. MY PICTURES.

"Three of them!" Beryl said. "Just in the four weeks I've been away. Tell me, are the kittens quite recovered?"

"Oh, yes. And the Edinburgh Rock was yummy. Thank you very much. But why did you send us a postcard with an elephant on it? Did you know that—"

"No, no," said Beryl. "I didn't know you'd seen a picture of an elephant, much less that you were going to wash one. It was simply that I was in a shop choosing a postcard and I was thinking about you and your pictures and something made me buy one with an elephant on it. I don't know why. Maybe we're on the same sort of wavelength, you and me."

"So you haven't got second-sight too?" said Sadie.

"Oh, no," said Beryl. "I can't see into the future; you're the one who can do that. But you may not always be able to, you know. Although you're the first person I've ever actually met who had these powers, I have read of other cases. Of children, I mean, who had the gift of foresight. Strangely enough, often in the Highlands. They're usually in their teens; I think you're the youngest I know of. But in all the cases I've read about, there was one thing in common."

"What was that?" Sadie asked.

"The children only possessed this power of second-sight for quite a short time."

"And then?"

"And then they somehow lost it. They couldn't see into the future any more, just as ordinary people can't. How long have you been seeing your pictures?"

"Since about the middle of last month, I think," Sadie said.

"For six weeks or so then," said Beryl. "And how many pictures have you seen altogether?"

Sadie began to count on her fingers. "Thunderstorm," she said. "One-pound coin. Nosebleed. The words 'Down Under'. You at the airport with your umbrella. The M4 pile-up. And then the three I just showed you. That's nine altogether."

"Would it worry you," Beryl said, "if you lost the gift? If you never saw any more pictures?"

"I don't know," Sadie said.

"I think," said Beryl, "that if I was you, I'd be quite glad. I don't really think I want to know what is going to happen in my future. I know that if I could foresee things, like you, it could be very useful. I mean, I might see a picture of a horse that was going to win a big race, and then I could put a lot of money on it and make a fortune. But the power could be very frightening and horrible."

"How do you mean?"

"I might foresee something awful happening to

someone I was fond of. Or to myself. And I'd know there was nothing I could do to stop it. Yes, I think I'm glad I haven't got second-sight."

They sat a while in silence, and then Sadie said, "I wish you weren't going back to Australia."

"I'll write to you," Beryl said, "and you must write to me and tell me all about every picture that you see. Promise?"

"Yes."

"And, like I said, when you're older perhaps you'll come to Australia one day, and maybe even get to see Abdul Pasha's wild cousins. You never know."

"Can I stay with you?"

"Of course."

When Beryl came to bed that night, Abdul Pasha had fallen out and was lying on the floor. Limp-humped and earless, he looked very old. Beryl picked him up and slipped him gently under Sadie's duvet, his head resting on the pillow. She stood looking down at the sleeper for a moment, and, though she smiled, she also sighed.

When she woke next morning, she saw that Sadie was sitting up in bed, reading.

"Any picture to tell me about, Sadie?" Beryl asked. "Last chance."

Sadie had indeed woken up with a picture in her mind, a very clear picture, but she felt she didn't want to tell her cousin about it. She didn't quite know why.

It was a picture of Beryl, standing (without an umbrella this time) in brilliant sunshine, outside a building that looked like an airport terminal. She could see a big notice on the front of the building that said,

QANTAS AIRLINES WELCOME YOU TO SYDNEY, CAPITAL OF NEW SOUTH WALES.

Her first thought had been – that's all right then; that's Beryl safely back in Australia. Yet Beryl seemed different. Sadie could see her clearly in the bright sunlight, and though she was still the same short tubby figure, her curly dark hair was streaked with grey and her face was much more lined and she wore spectacles.

Why it should be Sadie could not tell, but this Beryl in this picture suddenly looked ten years older. What could have happened to make her age like that?

"No pictures?" asked Beryl again.

Sadie shook her head. A bit better than telling a lie by saying "No" out loud, she thought.

"I think I'm glad," said Beryl. "After that business on the M4, I was half afraid you'd say you'd seen a picture of a plane crash."

"Oh, no," Sadie said. "You're going to get home all right, I'm sure of that."

Beryl smiled. "If you say so," she said.

On the way back from the zoo the previous day, Beryl had returned the white Vauxhall saloon to the car hire people; she had transferred herself and a number of parcels from the hire car to the Makepeaces' car.

At breakfast on the morning of her departure she gave these out. For Mr and Mrs Makepeace there were bottles of wine. For Carl there was a remote-control toy car. For Julia she had somehow managed to find a woolly kangaroo with a little woolly baby in its pouch.

She had even remembered the kittens. For each there was a tin of cat food, one partly fish, one mostly rabbit.

Sadie's present was a handsome blue-and-gold pen in a smart case.

"So that you can write to me when I'm back in Sydney," Beryl said to her, "and give me a picture of everything that's been happening," and she grinned at Sadie and Sadie grinned back.

And after breakfast it was time for Mr Makepeace to drive his Cousin Beryl to Heathrow.

She had said goodbye to everyone, even to old Abdul Pasha, and now, as the car pulled away, she wound down the window and called, "Au revoir!" It seemed to Sadie that she was saying it specially to her.

"What does 'au revoir' mean, Mum?" asked Sadie as the car disappeared from sight.

"It means 'till we meet again'."

"Do you think we ever will?"

"You never know."

Chapter 9

Ten Years On

Strangely, Sadie never saw another picture. That was the end of her second-sight.

Some weeks later a letter arrived from Down Under, thanking them for everything and saying how enjoyable the holiday had been. There was a postscript.

P.S. Don't forget to write, Sadie.

"Beryl seemed to take a great shine to Sadie, didn't she?" Brian Makepeace said to his wife.

"Yes. And vice versa. They seemed to be on the same wavelength."

Sadie did write back, with her new pen. "I haven't seen any pictures since you left," she wrote.

And six months later, a year later, she was still saying the same thing.

The years rolled by, and though there were times when Beryl wrote that she might come over again, and there were times when the Makepeaces considered taking a holiday in Australia, somehow something always cropped up to spoil their plans.

Until a particular letter arrived from Beryl shortly before Sadie's eighteenth birthday, when Carl was fourteen and a half, and Julia was almost eleven, and the youngest Makepeace, Colin, was nearly eight, the same age that Sadie had been when first she found out that she had second-sight. (How disappointed she was when she learned that her mother was to have another baby – she would have loved to have foreseen it: she couldn't have resisted telling her parents before they even knew themselves.)

Dear Brian and Jill, (the letter said)

    It seems such a long time (it is such a long time) since my holiday in the UK when I stayed with you. I still don't see my way to another visit – I seem to be so busy all the time – but I have a suggestion for you to consider.

    Sadie, if I reckon right, is shortly to be eighteen and thus "grown up". Do you think she would like to celebrate this milestone by coming to stay with me here in Sydney? I would take time off to show her around. I don't want to involve you in any expense, so I hope you will allow me to pay her return air fare.

As you know, I've never married, so never had children of my own, and I became very fond of Sadie all those years ago. I don't want to pressure you (or her) in any way, so I've not written to her. I'll leave it to you to sound her out (or, if you're dead against the idea, say nothing to her).

Love to you both, and the children, and to Partly and Mostly, if they still have some of their nine lives left, which I'm sure they do.

Beryl

Later that day Mr Makepeace said to the eldest of his four children, "How do you fancy a holiday abroad? You deserve one after all the work you've done for your A levels."

"And you won't know if you've got a university place until the results come out in August," said Sadie's mother, "so it's a good time to go."

"D'you mean a holiday for all of us?" Sadie asked.

"No, just you."

"Where?"

"Australia."

"Australia?"

"Yes. Beryl's invited you. You remember Cousin Beryl when she stayed here?"

"Yes, of course I do," said Sadie. "I must have been nearly eight, I should think. She was nice. Short and plump, with curly dark hair. I used to write to her quite a bit but I haven't for years now."

"Well, what do you think? Would you like to go to Australia?"

"Like to? I'd love to! It would be a fantastic experience. But what about the cost? The air fares must be very expensive."

"Beryl's paying."

"How wonderful!" said Sadie. "Can we ring her up, now, this very minute?"

"Later. It'll still be very early there – they're about ten hours ahead of us."

"And the bath-water goes down the plug-hole anticlockwise!" said Sadie. "I've never forgotten that, and never known whether Beryl was just joking. Now I'll be able to find out!"

At intervals during the long flight, Sadie thought about that strange, short time in her life when she had had second-sight. Or I believed I had, she said to herself. Beryl believed that some people could see into the future. But could I really? Or was it all dreaming? Did I just dream that those things were going to happen?

She tried to remember what it had felt like, all those years ago, to wake up in the morning with one of those clear pictures in her mind, but she couldn't really recall any of them properly.

Until, that is, the plane touched down at the end of the flight, and taxied towards the terminal building and stopped.

For when Sadie emerged from the plane, there was that big notice on the front of the building that said

QANTAS AIRLINES WELCOME YOU TO SYDNEY, CAPITAL OF NEW SOUTH WALES

QANTAS AIRLINES
WELCOMES YOU TO SYDNEY, CAPITAL OF NEW SOUTH WALES

and there was Beryl, standing waiting. Sadie could see her clearly in the bright sunlight, and though she was still the same short, tubby figure, her curly dark hair was streaked with grey and her face was much more lined and she wore spectacles.

"Sadie!" cried Beryl as they met and hugged. "How tall you are! Good job you waved at me – I'd never have recognized you."

"I recognized you straight away," said Sadie. "You look exactly the same."

Exactly the same, she thought, as you did in that last picture that I saw, ten years ago.

This is my second sight of it.